Ariane Dewey and Jose Aruego

SPLASH!

Green Light Readers
Clarion Books
An Imprint of HarperCollins*Publishers*
Boston New York

"Wake up, you big fur ball!" Nelly yelled.
She gave Sam a shake.

"Don't be a pest, Nelly," Sam growled.
"I'm dreaming about fat, floppy fish."
"Let's go find some!" Nelly said.

Nelly rushed out of their cave.
Sam jumped up and ran after her.

"Is that sound a splash?" asked Sam.
"I bet it's bears," said Nelly. "Let's hurry,
before all the fish are gone."

Together, they ran to the river.

The river was full of bears catching fish.
"Oh no," the bears groaned. "Here come
Sam and Nelly."

"What kind of mess will they
make this time?" said one bear.

Nelly slipped on a wet rock. She fell into the river. *Splash!*
"I'll save you!" Sam yelled, slipping after her.

Splash again!
Together, Nelly and Sam made a
wave that tipped over ten bears.

"Why are you two always so clumsy?"
growled one bear.
"We'll be more careful!" said Sam.

"OK, OK. You can fish with us," said the other bears. "But for once, try to behave."

Sam and Nelly sat very still with
the other bears. While they were
sitting, lots of fish swam by.

The bears had never seen so many fish
in one place. All they could hear was
the sound of swishing fins.

"Quick! Get them before they're gone!"
Sam yelled.
Hungry bears snapped at the fish.
The river was a jumble of fins and fur.
The bears had fun chasing the fish.

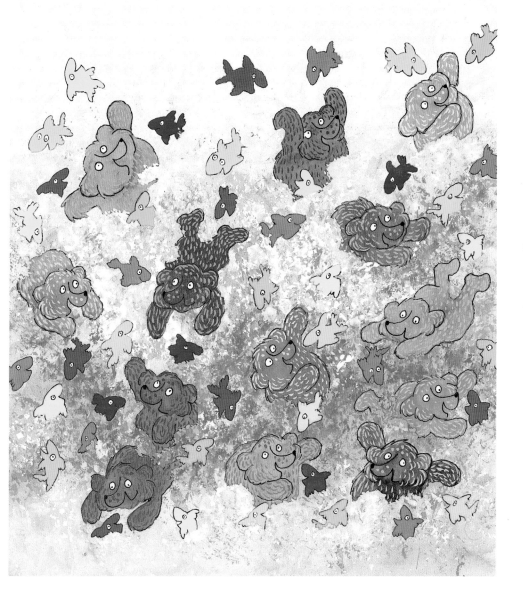

And the fish had fun racing away.
They swam to the bottom of a safe,
deep lake.

All of the bears had so much fun, they forgot they were hungry. Sam and Nelly walked home to their cave.

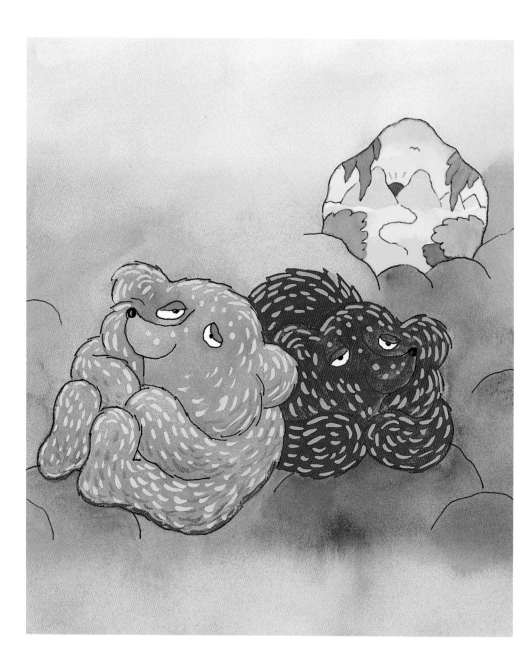

"We are clumsy," said Sam. "But we do have fun!" said Nelly. Now all they needed was a good long nap!

Think About It

1. Do you like Sam and Nelly? Why or why not?

2. How do the other bears feel about Nelly and Sam? How do you know?

3. What did the author-illustrators do to make the story funny?

Lift-the-Flap Science Book

**What do animals eat?
Make a book that shows
what one animal eats.**

WHAT YOU'LL NEED

paper   **crayons or markers**

scissors   **tape**

First, choose an animal. Find out what
that animal eats. Then follow these
steps to make a lift-the-flap book.

Bear
Food

1   Fold your paper in half. Write a title on the front.

what do bears eat?

2   Open the paper. Write a question asking what your animal eats.

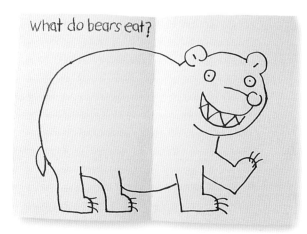

 Draw an outline of the animal's body.

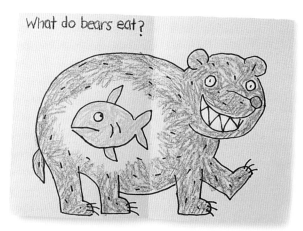

4 Now draw the food the animal eats in its stomach. Color the animal and the food.

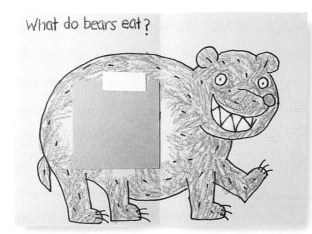

What do bears eat?

5 Cut a piece of paper to cover the food. Tape it over the food in your animal's stomach.

Bears eat fish.

6 Close the paper. On the back, write a sentence that tells what the animal eats.

Share your lift-the-flap book with a friend!

Meet the Author-Illustrators

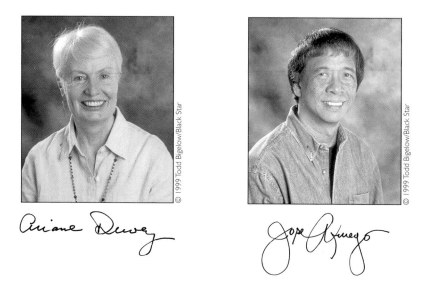

© 1999 Todd Bigelow/Black Star

© 1999 Todd Bigelow/Black Star

Ariane Dewey and Jose Aruego like working together. Jose loves to draw funny animals and Ariane loves to paint them. First, Jose draws the eyes. They show if the animal is happy, sad, mad, grumpy, or scared. Then he adds the ears, the nose, and the rest of the animal. When his drawings are finished, Ariane paints them in bright colors. Ariane and Jose hope the bears in *Splash!* make you smile.

clarionbooks.com

First Green Light Readers edition 2001
Green Light Readers is a trademark of HarperCollins Publishers LLC, registered in the
United States of America and/or other jurisdictions.

The Library of Congress has cataloged an earlier edition as follows:
Dewey, Ariane.
Splash!/by Ariane Dewey and Jose Aruego.
p.   cm.
"Green Light Readers."
Summary: Two clumsy bears join in fishing fun at the river.
[1. Bears—Fiction.   2. Clumsiness—Fiction.   3. Fishing—Fiction.]
I. Aruego, Jose.   II. Title.   III. Green Light Reader.
PZ7.D5228Sp   2001
[E]—dc21   00-9723
ISBN 978-0-15-204872-3
ISBN 978-0-15-204832-7 (pb)

22 SCP   20 19 18 17 16 15 14 13

Printed in China

Ages 5–7
Grade: 1–2
Guided Reading Level: G–I
Reading Recovery Level: 15–16

Green Light Readers
For the reader who's ready to GO!

"A must-have for any family with a beginning reader."—*Boston Sunday Herald*

"You can't go wrong with adding several copies of these terrific books to your beginning-to-read collection."—*School Library Journal*

"A winner for the beginner."—*Booklist*

Five Tips to Help Your Child Become a Great Reader

1. Get involved. Reading aloud to and with your child is just as important as encouraging your child to read independently.

2. Be curious. Ask questions about what your child is reading.

3. Make reading fun. Allow your child to pick books on subjects that interest her or him.

4. Words are everywhere—not just in books. Practice reading signs, packages, and cereal boxes with your child.

5. Set a good example. Make sure your child sees YOU reading.

Why Green Light Readers Is the Best Series for Your New Reader

• Created exclusively for beginning readers by some of the biggest and brightest names in children's books

• Reinforces the reading skills your child is learning in school

• Encourages children to read—and finish—books by themselves

• Offers extra enrichment through fun, age-appropriate activities unique to each story

• Incorporates characteristics of the Reading Recovery program used by educators

• Developed with Harcourt School Publishers and credentialed educational consultants